by **Lesléa Newman**

**Illustrations by**
**Peter Ferguson**

# The Boy Who Cried
# *fabulous*

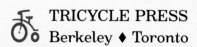
TRICYCLE PRESS
Berkeley ♦ Toronto

When Roger started out for school,
his mother set a simple rule.

She said, "Now Roger, you go straight—
*straight* to class, and don't be late."

Roger tried hard to obey,
he knew that he should not delay.

He shouldn't wander or explore
but then he came upon a store,
its windows full of lovely clothes
so colorful that Roger froze,
then clapped his hands in fits of glee
and shouted out in ecstasy:

"What a fabulous coat,
is it silk or wool?
What a fabulous bell,
can I give it a pull?

What a fabulous door,
does it open wide?
What a fabulous store,
can I come inside?

"What a fabulous man
in a fabulous hat.
What a fabulous tie,
or perhaps a cravat?

What a fabulous boot,
what a fabulous shoe.
What a fabulous suit
made of fabulous blue.

What a fabulous dog,
what a fabulous cat.
What a fabulous this,
what a fabulous that.

What a fabulous boy,
what a fabulous girl.

What a fabulous day,
what a fabulous world!"

Roger got to school so late,
his teacher was in quite a state.

He said to Roger,

This is bad.

And I am

very, VERY

mad.

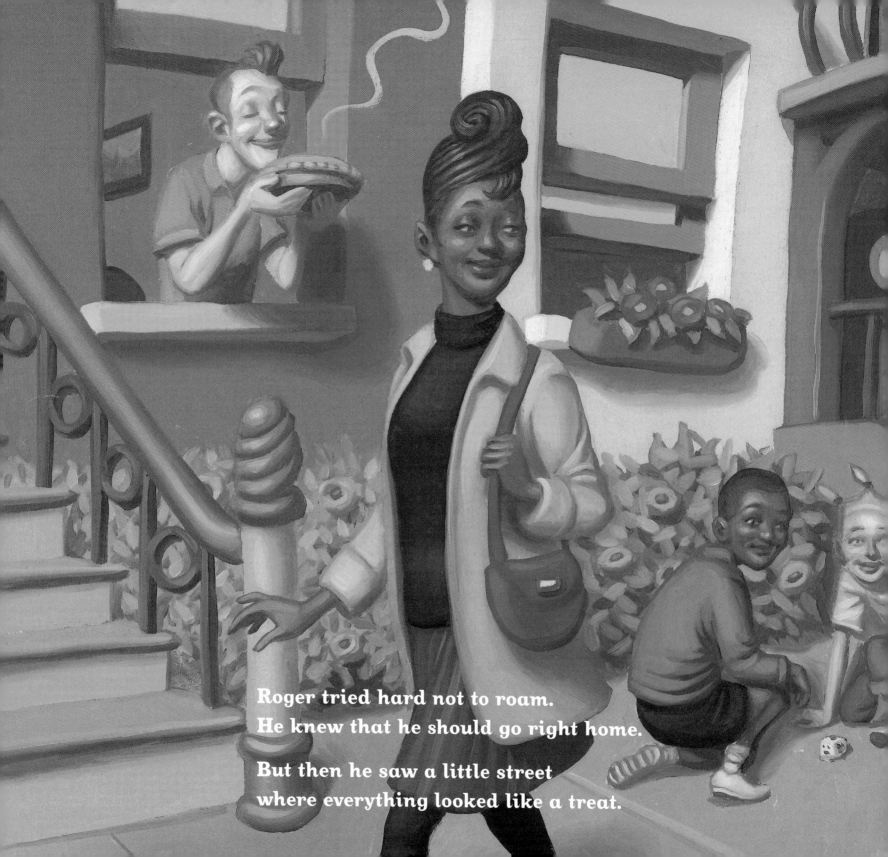

Roger tried hard not to roam.
He knew that he should go right home.

But then he saw a little street
where everything looked like a treat.

So many colors, such a sight,
it made him shriek with pure delight:

"What a fabulous pie,
can I have a slice?
What a fabulous game,
can I roll the dice?

What a fabulous book,
can I read a line?
What a fabulous purse,
it's simply divine!

What a fabulous ball,
what a fabulous bike.
What a fabulous day
for a fabulous hike.

What a fabulous lake,
what a fabulous park.
What a fabulous sky,
it's so fabulously
### dark!"

Roger's mom was very sad.
Behind her stood his angry dad.

"Roger you are very late."
"But Mom, but Dad," said Roger. "Wait."

"I know that I am not on time.
But what I did was not a crime.

With so many fabulous things to see,
the time just got away from me."

Roger's mother shook her head.
Roger's dad sent him to bed.

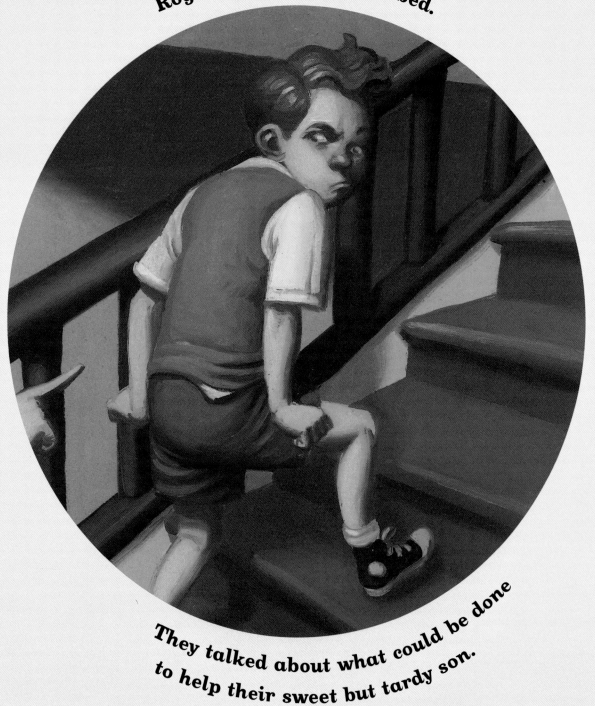

They talked about what could be done
to help their sweet but tardy son.

"If he kept his eyes upon the ground and did not stop to look around,

surely he'd pick up the pace, and swiftly move from place to place."

The next day Mom said, "Roger dear,
there's one word we don't want to hear."

"Now son," said Dad, "listen to us.
We're talking about *fabulous*.

Now come along, we're off to town
and please remove that silly frown."

Roger tried hard to be good.
He wanted to, he knew he should.

He also knew one thing for sure—
the world's too wondrous to ignore.

And so he found another way

to shout out what he had to say:

"What a **marvelous** watch,
can I see the time?
What a marvelous drink,
does it need a lime?

What a marvelous dish,
what a marvelous brunch.
What a marvelous place
for a marvelous lunch.

"What a wonderful bridge,
what a beautiful boat.
What an elegant queen
on a dazzling float.

What a glorious band,
what a magical song.
What a splendid march,
may we come along?

"What a luscious smell
in the scrumptious air.
What a stunning day
for a charming fair.

What a thrilling show,
what a brilliant clown.
What a magnificent street,
what a **fabulous** town!"

Roger felt his spirits dim,
as both his parents looked at him.

But then they smiled with such delight,
he knew that it would be all right.

"We've never, ever had such fun,
and you are the world's most fabulous son!"

For Roger Grodsky,
the boy who cried fabulous
—LN

Tricycle Press
*a little division of Ten Speed Press*
P.O. Box 7123
Berkeley, California 94707
www.tenspeed.com

Book design by Betsy Stromberg
Typeset in Oxtail

Library of Congress Cataloging-in-Publication Data
Newman, Lesléa.
  The boy who cried fabulous / by Lesléa Newman ; illustrated by
Peter Ferguson.
     p. cm.
Summary: A young boy's fascination with everything he sees
around him causes him to be late and upsets his parents, until they
come to realize his special gift.
  ISBN 1-58246-101-5
  [1. Conduct of life--Fiction. 2. Happiness--Fiction. 3. Tardiness--
Fiction. 4. Parent and child--Fiction. 5. Stories in rhyme.]
I. Ferguson, Peter, 1968- ill. II. Title.
PZ8.3.N4655Bo 2004
[E]--dc22                                              2003017054

First Tricycle Press printing, 2004
Printed in Singapore

1 2 3 4 5 6 — 08 07 06 05 04